MASK™

VOLCANO
OF VENOM

The hum of the two MASK vehicles could be heard across the still, hot summer air as the Rhino and Gator sped towards the Mexican Border.

"There have been no further reports of earthquakes," Matt Trakker informed his team-mates, Bruce Sato and Hondo Maclean, through the MASK radios.

"Let's hope we can stop the vibro-machines before VENOM can do any more damage," replied Maclean as they drew close to Mount Carmel, the volcano at the centre of the recent troubles.

"VENOM is inside that volcano," Matt said as he scanned the area for signs of danger.

"You know it's a VENOM trap," Hondo said in his school teacher voice, as if he was trying to coax a reluctant pupil into admitting something.

"Yes," Matt answered, "but if we don't take the bait they'll use their machine to destroy the nearby towns by making the volcano erupt."

As they entered the eerie mouth of the tunnel each member of the MASK team was aware that VENOM — and especially its ruthless leader, Miles Mayhem — wouldn't have forced them to come here unless he had made plans for this to be their last trip. "Let's get this over with," Hondo encouraged, "we have a date with VENOM."

"I knew that do-gooder Trakker couldn't refuse to come here once I made him an offer he couldn't say no to," sneered Miles Mayhem as he watched the progress of the trio of MASK agents on one of his many video screens. "Energise defence systems," he told his evil henchman, Sly Rax.

"Trakker has to use that tunnel, boss," Rax confirmed as he flicked the necessary switches on the control panels, "and we have it booby-trapped every inch of the way."

A cold, calculating grin grew across Mayhem's face as he watched the MASK team walk deeper into his trap.

The detectors inside the masks worn by Matt and friends told them that they were being watched. For the moment, however, there was no point in letting Mayhem know how much they knew about his operation. They would just bide their time until it was right — and then they would strike.

Unless VENOM struck first! As soon as Matt felt the ground begin to give way he tried to shift his weight . . . but it was too late. The ground crumbled away underfoot to reveal a deep pit leading downward to a bed of razor-sharp spikes!

As Matt fell, Sato activated his Lifter Mask and, catching him in its special rays, lifted the MASK leader out of danger. "Thanks, Bruce," gasped Matt. "I'm lucky VENOM made such a deep pit. The extra time it took to fall gave you the time needed to rescue me."

"VENOM is too evil for its own good," Sato replied in his usual style of double meanings.

Mayhem's face began to turn red with anger as he watched the rescue on his vid-screen. "Bah!" he exploded, "I hate their pesky masks! But they'll need more than mere masks to stop this . . ." As Mayhem finished speaking his left thumb pressed a yellow button on his console.

As soon as the signal was passed from the console a giant flying ram was activated. Within moments it was hurtling towards Matt and friends.

"Mayhem's not giving us much breathing space," Hondo observed as the metallic missile sped towards them.

"This one's mine," continued Hondo as he activated his Blaster Mask. Immediately, a stream of energy-bolts shot from his visor and shattered the ram with a terrific KER-BAM!

"Things are beginning to warm up," Matt commented as they bravely walked on.

For the next several hundred metres nothing happened. Then they came into a section of the tunnel in which the side became very narrow with less than a three metres gap between the walls.

"If ever I saw a place to set a trap it is here," Hondo said as they slowed their pace down.

"You're right," Matt confirmed, "so let's keep our eyes and ears open."

"What's that noise?" Sato asked as a low hum began to sound around them.

"I don't know . . . but I don't like it," replied Matt as he eyed the rocky features of the walls.

Suddenly Hondo called out, "The walls! Look at the walls!"

As Bruce and Matt looked at the rocky sides of the tunnel their hearts missed a beat . . . the walls were closing in on them!

Mayhem's cold, evil eyes watched the walls slowly close together on his vid-screen. Finally, when nothing remained but the slightest of gaps, he allowed a grin to split across his face.

"There were no shots . . . nothing. It would be impossible for MASK to survive that trap." As Mayhem realised this, his deep, cackling laugh echoed around the control room.

The evil Mayhem's laughter was short-lived, however. For as the walls slid back, Mayhem was stunned to see that somehow the MASK agents had escaped! "Gone!" Mayhem shouted as he slammed his fist into the side of the console.

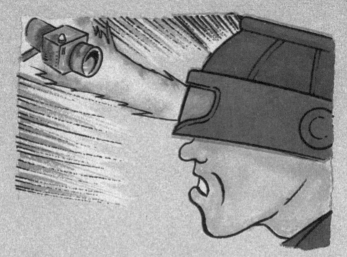

As soon as the walls moved back Hondo raised his head from under the soft ground and fired a blaster-bolt at the camera lens on the ceiling.

"It was quick thinking to use your blaster to dig a trench for us to hide in," praised Matt as he and Sato began to crawl out of the ground.

"And with his camera smashed Mayhem will never know how we did it," smirked Sato.

A short distance on, the tunnel widened once more to its original width. Before the MASK agents began to feel any safer, however, another deadly menace revealed itself.

From out of the wall appeared several laser guns which began to fire at the MASK team. Only the super-quick reactions of Sato saved them as he used his Lifter Mask to raise rocks in front of them to shield the heroic team from the deadly beams!

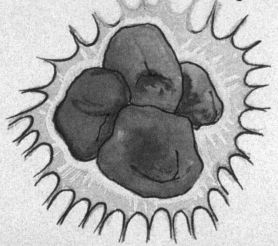

"I didn't think they could get this far," Mayhem confessed to Sly Rax, "but I still planned for that possibility."

"Your line of explosives?" suggested Rax.

Mayhem's smile told Rax that his guess had been right. "I press this button," Mayhem explained, pointing to a row of buttons, "and MASK will be just a sad memory."

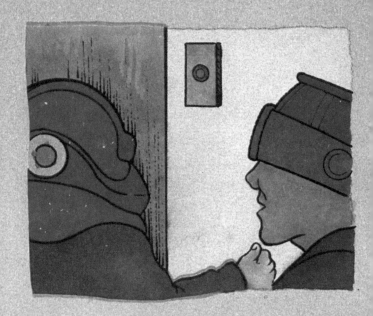

As Mayhem's finger touched the button, a small box was energised in the tunnel. "As soon as MASK break the electric beam emitted from the box it will explode," Mayhem boasted to Rax, who nodded in approval.

"My mask has just picked up a signal," Matt said, pointing towards a small metal box in the tunnel.

"It looks like some kind of detonator," observed Hondo, who knew a great deal about these things.

"I'll use my Ultra-flash to set it off," stated Matt as he fired a beam of high-energy light at the box.

Immediately the tunnel was full of light and noise. As the box detonated a series of bombs scattered around the tunnel. Because MASK were standing so far away from the bombs they were protected by their suits. As the smoke began to clear Sato noticed something remarkable had happened and called to Matt.

"Look, Matt," shouted Sato, "the explosion has opened a second tunnel."

"Great," replied Matt. "Since Mayhem never thought we would be using it he wouldn't have booby trapped it. So we can use it as a safe passageway to his headquarters."

Within moments the MASK team were in the safer, newly discovered tunnel. At least they were now out of danger from Mayhem's traps.

"Looks like this tunnel is leading right to the heart of the volcano," Hondo said as the trio began to move along the passageway.

"And that should lead us to Mayhem," concluded Matt.

By this time, Mayhem was overcome with anger. "MASK have done it again," he ranted, "but they haven't won yet. Before we desert this headquarters we'll detonate the bombs in the volcano's core."

Deciding to kill two birds with his single stone, Mayhem ordered that Rax and he would make their escape along the same tunnel MASK were using. "This will allow us a last shot at them as we leave," he explained to Rax.

"And if that fails," Rax answered, "we have just set the timing device on the bombs!"

"Company!" hollered Hondo, as he heard the approaching sound of the Switchblade and Piranha.

MASK just had time to take cover behind the rocks in the tunnel before the VENOM vehicles sped into view. Instantly laser and mask-fire shattered the stillness of the tunnel.

Sato and Matt combined their masks' powers to bring a section of the tunnel roof crashing down, forcing VENOM to retreat back to the control room. Before VENOM could close the security doors behind them, MASK smashed their way into the control room.

"But where's Mayhem?" Sato asked as the agents searched the now empty control room.

"I'm right here," announced Mayhem as he, Rax and Dagger burst into the room. Immediately the room was covered in a criss-cross of mask fire. Because of the sudden surprise created by Mayhem's attack, MASK were slowly forced into a small side-room.

Once inside, MASK were pinned down behind a large console as VENOM firepower sprayed the room with explosions and blasts. Even in the heat of the battle, Matt's eyes were searching the room for whatever information he could use to turn the tables on VENOM.

At the same moment, two interesting things happened: firstly the VENOM agents called off their attack and followed Mayhem away from the room. Secondly, Matt spotted that a timer on one of the machines had started. It now read: VOLCANO DETONATION 4.08.

"The whole volcano's set to blow," Matt informed the others.

Before anyone could reply they heard a loud mechanical sound. When they looked into the large control room they found that one of the walls had rolled down and that the VENOM vehicles were escaping.

"He's high-tailing it while he still has time," Hondo commented to Matt.

"Yes, but that's the least of our problems now," Matt said as he looked at the timer. "We have just under four minutes," he announced.

"Just long enough to boil an egg," Hondo replied, as he walked over to the mainframe computer against the wall.

Hondo tried to stop the countdown through the computer, but found it impossible. "Mayhem's locked everything out of the computer," he reported to Matt.

"Then we'll have to go inside ourselves," Sato said as he began to unscrew the back of the main computer. Within seconds he was surrounded with wires and chipboards.

"We're down to less than a minute," Hondo informed Sato as the design wizard cut and re-joined various wires in the back of the computer.

"I'm putting it back together now," Sato told Hondo, "once I input 'stop' it should turn off the bomb."

Hondo knew exactly what would happen to MASK and the local towns if Sato failed . . . KA-POW!

"Ready," informed Sato as he sat
down at the keyboard of the computer.
His quick, well-practised fingers typed
the word 'stop' on the keyboard. Now
all they could do was watch the
countdown on the timer. If it reached
zero all was lost!

"Nothing's happening," Hondo said in a hushed voice, as he watched the timer drop from 15 to 14 to 13. . . . Then a loud 'click' was heard and everything stopped. The low hum that had been in the background all the time stopped, as did the counter, with just seven seconds to spare!

"Our job's done here," Matt said when they all began to breathe again and had finished slapping Sato on the back for a job well done. "We have beaten VENOM once more, and saved the local towns from his volcano weapon."

"The next time," Hondo said, "let us do it with a bit more time to spare!"

And with that they set off for America and home.